don't
now

HAIRCUT and
JUST A NIBBLE

PAUL JENNINGS and ANDREW WELDON

Text copyright © Lockley Lodge Pty, Ltd, 2013
Illustrations, diagrams, handmade fonts copyright © Andrew Weldon, 2013

First published in Australia by Allen & Unwin, 2013
This edition published in 2015
by Hodder Children's Books

Designed by Andrew Weldon and Bruno Herfst

A Catalogue record for this book is available from the British Library

ISBN 978 1 444 92127 4

MIX
Paper from
responsible sources
FSC® C104740

The paper and board used in this book are made from wood from responsible
sources.

Hodder Children's Books
A division of Hachette Children's Group
Part of Hodder & Stoughton
Hachette UK Limited
Carmelite House, 50 Embankment, London EC4Y 0DZ

www.hachette.co.uk

SAMANTHA'S YARD ©RICKY ™

DOG'S WET NOSE - GOOP, SLOBBER, ETC

CHEWED-UP DOG TOYS

WORF! WORF! WORF! WORF! WORF! WORF! WORF!

THEIR SERIOUSLY YAPPY DOG

DOG-HOUSE

HUMAN HOUSE

VIEW PRETTY MUCH INTO THEIR LOUNGE ROOM. NOT THAT I'M LOOKING.

DOG PLAY AREA - TREAD CAREFULLY IF YOU KNOW WHAT I MEAN

CAMPFIRE

SAMANTHA'S CLOTHES

SAMANTHA'S POOL WATER

POOL (WHERE SAMANTHA SWIMS SOMETIMES PROBABLY)

SAMANTHA'S BEACH BALL

I GUESS SAMANTHA LIES ON THIS

POSSIBLE SPOT FOR CONNECTING DOOR?

OUR TREE

HER TREE

OUR SHED

OUR HOUSE

STORY ONE

HAIR CUT

1
THE CLOWN

Normally I wouldn't get stuck in the car with Dad. Don't get me wrong, I love him.But he always takes the opportunity to give me a lecture. And there is no escape. I can't just pretend to go off and clean up my bedroom.

I am trapped.

Of course, I could use my secret power and fly off.

But I wouldn't even be able to get off the ground with Dad looking at me.

I stared out the window and tried not to listen as our car crept forward.

'You need a haircut,' said Dad. 'You look like the top of a mop.'

I didn't answer. My feelings were hurt.

Okay, I admit it. I am not perfect. The mirror tells no lies. I am a dork and I look like one.

But I was not going to follow Dad's fashion advice. He sometimes wore sandals with socks. I wouldn't be seen dead doing that.

There was a photo of Dad at home where he had a ponytail right down to his waist.

I was always scared that he would grow it again.
And people would see me with him.

'You should get it styled,' said Dad. 'Like mine.
Nice and neat.'

'And thin,' I said.

That's what I was thinking about at the very
moment when it all started. Hair. Mine was short
and scruffy. Nice and casual.

I wouldn't change it for Mum. I wouldn't change
it for Dad. I wouldn't change it for...

I never finished the thought. Something else put
it right out of my mind.

There she was again. The girl who lived next door to us. It was definitely her. Samantha. Sitting warming herself in the sun. Her father worked at the car wash.

I really liked her, but she didn't even know that I existed. I was lonely. I wanted a friend. And I wanted it to be her. If I was honest I had to admit that I more than liked her.

This time she wasn't listening to her headphones. She was talking on her phone.

I gave her a nod, but she ignored me. Maybe the sun was in her eyes. But she was wearing sunglasses so that couldn't be it. Maybe she just didn't like boys.

We moved forward slowly until our car was next.

I wound my window down so that I could hear what Samantha was talking about on the phone.

'Jack is such a sweetheart,' she said. 'I really, really, really love him. He's amazing. So clever.'

What? She had a boyfriend. At her age. I didn't know why I was surprised because she had a lot going for her. She had a beautiful singing voice. And the face to go with it.

I nodded at her again, but as usual she ignored me and kept talking on her phone. I could hear every word.

'I love Jack's long hair. It makes me shiver all over when I touch it. And I love the way he nibbles my ear.'

Oh, what? I couldn't bear to hear about this kid Jack. I wondered what he looked like. Long hair? He had long hair? And she liked it.

As Dad drove the car into the car wash I started to form a picture in my mind.

I could just imagine him.

HOW I IMAGINED **JACK**

- <u>That</u> hair. ————————

- Mysterious eyes. ————

- Probably not a nail-chewer. —

- Annoyingly confident. ——

- Older, undoubtedly. ———

- General superiority. ——

'Put that window up and stop daydreaming,' said Dad.

I wasn't listening. I was thinking about Jack and his long hair. And how Samantha loved him. She was laughing and smiling while she talked about him.

There was no point in denying it.

I was jealous.

'Were you ever in love when you were a boy?'
I said to Dad.

I wanted him to give me some advice. I wanted
him to tell me what to do.

'Yes,' he said. 'She had red hair.'

'What did you do?' I said.

He didn't answer.

He was in a world of his own.

I had to do something. I had to impress Samantha.

I had to show her that I wasn't a dork.

I had to get her attention.

I was the only boy in the world who could fly.

But I couldn't fly when anyone was looking.

I would fall to my death if even a dog saw me.

Dad was still dreaming about some long-lost love.

So I did it.

I put on a show for Samantha.

I gave it my all. I did every trick I could think of.

Okay, so my tricks didn't work. Samantha didn't even notice me.

As we left the car wash she was still raving on about Jack and his lovely hair.

We drove home in silence.

I had made a total idiot of myself. And Dad and I both knew it.

Dad didn't say anything for a bit. Then he gave a little smile.

'You were showing off,' he said. 'That's no way to get a girl. You have to show her that you care.'

'I can't,' I said.

'Why not?'

Because I'm…

Girls would never listen to me. They didn't like
me. And none of my tricks had worked. The only
way I could impress anyone at all was to fly.

If people knew that I could fly, everything would be different.

If people knew I could fly, no one would think I was a dork.

If people knew I could fly, girls would talk to me.

If people knew I could fly, the shyness would fall away like an old coat dropping to the floor.

I would be…

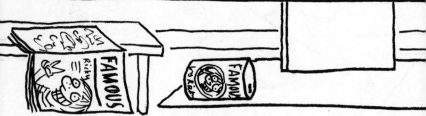

'You have to care,' Dad said again. 'That's what matters. Don't show off. Do something kind. Make her happy. Even if she doesn't know about it. Then, in the end, it will all work out for the best.'

I gave a weak smile. I didn't believe him. I had to get Samantha's attention. I had to do something to make her notice me.

2
LOOKING BAD

Okay, so Jack had long hair. I could beat him at that. Yes, that was it. I would do whatever it took to grow long, sleek hair.

It took a long time for hair to grow. A really long time. I checked it as soon as we got back from the car wash. Every day I looked in the mirror, but nothing seemed to be happening. I even measured it with a ruler. Not even a millimetre a day. Nothing.

HAIR-GROWING STRATEGIES

SQUEEZE IT OUT

EAT HEAPS OF VEGIES

PULL

WATER REGULARLY

FERTILISER

SHRINK HEAD
(NOT REALLY PRACTICAL)

I decided to ask Dad for advice again when we were having breakfast one morning. But he wasn't much help.

'You know that redhead you were telling me about?' I said.

'I don't remember any redhead,' he mumbled.

'I do,' said Mum in a cross voice. 'Beautiful red hair.'

'I always liked your hair better,' said Dad. 'It was, er, is wonderful. You really didn't have to buy that wig.'

'Your father liked girls with red hair,' said Mum. 'So I bought a wig.'

'A wig?' I yelled. 'Where is it now?'

'In the shed,' said Mum. 'With all of Grandad's junk.'

'Can I have it?' I asked.

'No,' said Dad.

'Yes,' said Mum. 'You're welcome to it. It was a cheap, horrible thing anyway. It made me look like a hippy.'

'Let's talk about something else,' said Dad.

Later that day I went outside and made a beeline for the shed. As I got closer, I heard the sound of voices coming over the wall. Girls' voices. They were laughing and giggling. I could hear the sound of water splashing.

Samantha.

It was her house. She was there with her

girlfriends. I wondered what they were doing.

I was very tempted to fly up to the top of the

wall and take a peek. But if any of them saw me

I would drop like a stone. I had already broken

my leg once before when I was seen up there.

It was too dangerous.

I went into the shed and started sorting

through the junk. It was mainly Dad's neat and

tidy workshop, but the back was full of junk.

There sure was a lot of it. Old bikes, tins, jars

of nails, chairs, a dog collar, a broken bed,

a dusty washbasin and Grandad's toenail

clippings. Cobwebs were everywhere.

I lifted boxes around and crawled into spaces.

I was covered in grime. And the place stank.

Soon I was on the nose myself. It was terrible.

Then I saw something. A pile of rags. A hairy pile.

No, it wasn't rags.

It was the wig.

I grabbed it and gave it a shake. A cloud of choking dust floated in the air and made me cough.

The wig was red. More of an afro style than long, but not too bad. Maybe sort of cool. I pulled it on.

I wondered what I looked like.

I scanned the shed for a mirror. Nothing.
I wondered if this wig would do the trick with
Samantha. Would she like my new look?

There was only one way to find out.

I went outside and stared at the top of the wall.
I decided to take the risk.

'Up,' I said.

I spotted a leafy tree growing on the other side. I flew along our side of the wall and then up to the top.

There were about twenty girls in Samantha's backyard. They all wore light-blue shirts and dark-blue skirts. They had heaps of badges sewn onto sashes. Some wore whistles around their necks. Most of them had Swiss Army knives on their belts.

HENRIETTA
SCHWARTZ

DAISY
LI

FLORINDA
JELLY

JUANITA
SANCHEZ

THERESA
LOUISA
DOPPLE

DESDEMONA
DONALDSON

They were Girl Guides. And Samantha was one
of them. I noticed that she didn't have any badges.
She was a new girl. She mustn't have earned any
badges yet.

A tall woman seemed to be in charge. The leader
of the pack. She was an old lady of about thirty.

'Now then, girls,' said the leader. 'All quiet while Jennifer finishes off the last task for her Lifesaving badge.'

Jennifer was wearing green bathers. She walked to the edge of the pool.

'Go,' yelled the leader.

Jennifer dived into the pool. I could see her shadowy figure swimming deeper and deeper. The seconds ticked by. She was a blur on the bottom of the pool. Everyone was silent.

Was she in trouble?

No.

All of the girls went crazy. They yelled and cheered as she climbed out of the pool carrying the brick she had grabbed from the bottom.

The girls formed a circle, with the leader and Jennifer standing in the middle. The leader handed Jennifer a small patch.

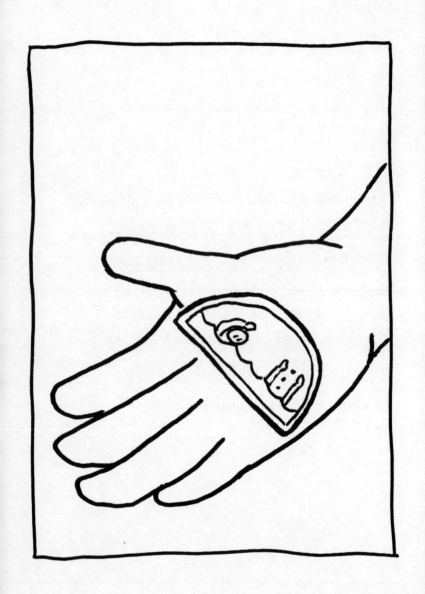

'Congratulations,' she said. 'I am pleased to award Jennifer her Lifesaving Award. She can add this to all her other badges.' All the girls clapped.

Jennifer had earned her Lifesaving badge.
I wondered what other badges they could get.
The girls had a lot of badges.

B A D

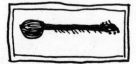

LIFESAVING

FIRE LIGHTING

TYING KNOTS

UNTYING KNOTS

ESPERANTO

SARCASM

NOSE MAINTENANCE

YELLING

SNAKE-VENOM MILKING

SITAR

G E S

PIMPLE
CAMOUFLAGE

PET GROOMING

TAXIDERMY

SUMO

YOYO

IMPERSONATION

TWO-FINGER
WHISTLING

LINT REMOVAL

CLAPPER
LOADING

'And,' said the leader, 'now that Jennifer has twenty badges she is entitled to wear this on her belt.'

That's when I noticed that Samantha was the only other girl without a Swiss Army knife. It wasn't fair.

At that very moment it started to rain. Water trickled down my face. It was time for me to go. Before someone spotted me.

But I was too late. Loud voices filled the air.

'There's someone sitting on the wall,' said one of the girls.

'Who is it?'

'A clown.'

There was dead silence. Then...

They hooted and screamed. Tears ran down their faces. They yelled rude comments and pinched their noses with their fingers.

'Look.'

'Freakazoid.'

'Creep.'

'Weirdo.'

Their words made me feel bad. But Samantha's

voice was the one that hurt me most.

'It must be the boy next door,' she said. 'I've heard he's a bit strange.'

3
LOOKING GOOD

I quickly wriggled off the wall and hung on our side by my fingertips. No one could see me. It was safe for me to fly.

'Down,' I said.

I let go of the wall and gently floated to the ground.

I rushed inside and looked at myself in the mirror.

The girls were right.

I was a freak. A monster.

Red dye ran down through the dust on my face. It looked like rivers of blood. I was a horrible sight. There was only one word to describe me.

Idiotic.

I threw the stupid wig on the floor and stared into the mirror. I held up my right hand and spoke to my reflection.

I took a vow.

'I will not go anywhere near Samantha until my own hair has grown down past my shoulders.'

I knew that she would like me when she saw my long hair. But just to be on the safe side, there was something else I could do for her.

I walked over to my desk.

I turned my Swiss Army knife over in my hand.

I could see why all the Guides had them. Very

useful if you were lost in the bush.

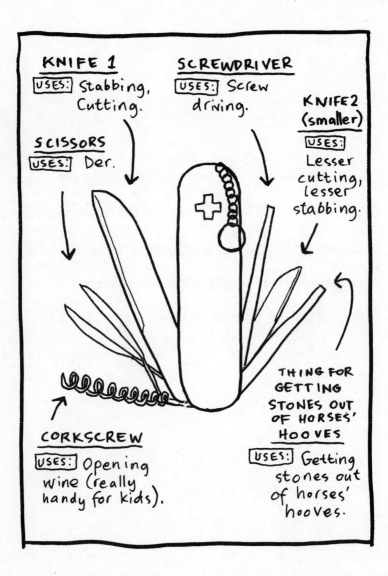

When my hair was long, when Samantha was my best friend, I would give it to her for her birthday.

I smiled. Things would work out. I just knew they would.

But first things first. My hair.

Every day I checked it.

I combed it and brushed it. I kept it clean and
shiny. I really wanted to impress Samantha
with it.

'When are you going to cut your hair?' Mum
asked.

'Never,' I said.

'What do the kids at school think of it?' asked Dad.

'Some teased me at first,' I said. 'But they got
into trouble. Our school has a strict no-bullying
policy.'

'Perhaps we should have a talk,' said Dad.

He wanted us to meet at our spot on top
of the roof.

I shook my head.

There were some things that were private. My
hairstyle was one of them. And Samantha was
another. If she became my friend, I wouldn't
care what anyone else thought.

Anyway, it was all going to be over before long.

I had already made up my mind what I'd do.

I knew she would be impressed by my hair.

But something happened before I could follow through with my plan.

I was lying in bed when I heard noises.

Something was going on in Samantha's backyard.

I could hear laughing and shouting. Girls' voices.

The Guides were back.

There was no way I was going up on that wall again. They would think I was a creep. That I was spying on them. I would have to go up to the front door and knock. It was the right thing to do.

It was dark outside, and cold. I wondered how Samantha was keeping warm.

I pulled the blanket up over my head and tried to drown out the sounds from Samantha's place. I switched off the light and pulled my doona over my head.

But it was no good.

Terrible thoughts crept into my mind.

I tried to push the thoughts out of my head. But I couldn't. I had to know if his hair was as good as mine. I had to see what was going on. I had to see if Jack was there.

I jumped out of bed and got dressed.

Then I pulled on my hoodie. I would be hard to see in the dark. I could fly up over the wall and I would be safe. There was no moon. The sky was black. It felt like rain was coming, and if anyone looked up they wouldn't see a thing. I would just take a quick peek. There was nothing wrong with that.

In no time at all I was over the fence.

The first thing I noticed was that Jack wasn't there.

I wasn't going to get a look at my rival.

Just the girls, the leader and Samantha's dog.

I hoped the dog wasn't going to look up and see me. Dogs have good eyesight. If it saw me I would fall to the ground and die.

Samantha was in the centre of the group. Even though I was flying high, I could hear their voices bouncing off the brick wall around the backyard.

'Three matches left,' said their leader. 'Go slowly. You can do it, Samantha!'

I saw a small flare of light. It blazed for a second and then died.

A low wail of disappointment came from the girls.

'Let me help,' said one of the girls.

'No,' said Samantha. 'I can do it on my own, thanks.'

It was hard for me to see. She was doing something with the twigs. And I heard the rustle of paper.

Suddenly I realised what was happening. She was trying to light a fire. She must be going for her Campfire badge.

'Ouch,' yelled Samantha. The flame bounced across the ground and died. She had burnt her fingers.

'Two matches left,' said the leader.

Samantha fumbled with the box.

At that very moment I felt something on my head.

I pulled my hoodie tightly around my face and gave a shiver.

'It's raining,' I heard someone say. 'She will never get it lit now.'

'It's not fair,' said another voice. 'I'm going to help her.'

'No,' I heard Samantha call out. 'I want to do it on my own. Everyone else has. I don't want special help.'

'But it's raining. The paper is wet.'

Another match flared and died.

'Let's go inside, girls,' said the leader. 'You can do it another day. When it's not raining.'

'No,' said Samantha.

'Yes,' said the leader. 'Come on, girls. Quick sticks. Inside before you all get wet and catch colds.' She took Samantha's hand and pulled her to her feet.

The girls headed into the house. The leader held Samantha's hand as they walked towards the door. She held onto her hand firmly. She wasn't going to let Samantha go until they were inside.

4
THE LAST MATCH

My brain was burning. This was terrible.

This was unfair. Samantha was the only girl with no badges. She didn't even have a Swiss Army knife.

And it was raining. They should have let her have another ten matches because the paper was wet.

I had to do something.

And I did.

'Down,' I said.

I dropped through the air more quickly than
I should have. I was in a hurry. I landed next
to the unlit campfire with a jolt. I felt the bones
in my legs shudder, but I was all right. Nothing
was broken.

I bent over the fire. If I could get it going, the
girls would see it and think that a spark from
Samantha's matches had set it ablaze.

The paper was wet. The twigs were wet.
I looked around for something to get the fire
going. I had to hurry.

Samantha had dropped the box of matches when the leader took her inside. I had to be careful. I only had one chance.

I was good at some things. But lighting fires wasn't one of them.

I stared at the wet paper and the little pile of twigs. I needed some dry paper. I looked around the yard.

Nothing, nothing, nothing.

Think, think, think.

What could I do?

Yes, yes, yes.

No, no, no.

I couldn't.

I could.

I took out my Swiss Army knife and opened
the scissors.

In the end, sparks and flames were shooting into the cold, wet air. 'Look,' screamed one of the girls. They all rushed to the window.

I quickly darted behind a bush. If they saw me, all would be lost. I ducked down and crawled around the side of the house. Then, unseen, I slowly lifted into the air. I heard the girls shouting excitedly. They had seen the fire.

'You did it, Samantha.'

'Yahoo.'

'Awesome, no one has ever done it in the rain before.'

The leader came outside and stood by the fire, staring down. Then she looked around the garden. I could tell she was suspicious.

Finally she walked back towards the house.

She took something out of her pocket.

The girls were crowded at the door.

'This is for you, Samantha,' said the leader.

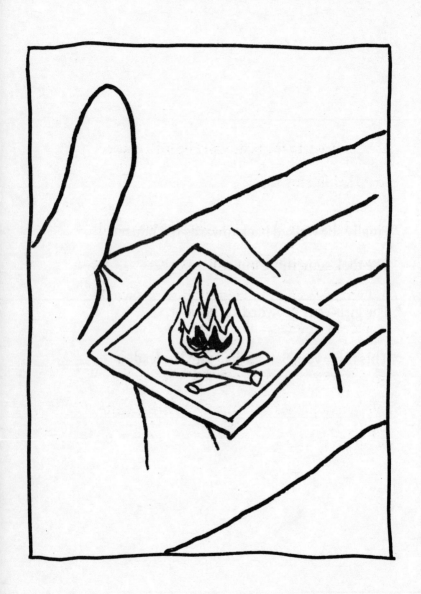

As I flew back to my bedroom I heard a cheer
go up behind me.

I would never be able to tell anyone what I had
done. If Samantha found out, she would feel bad
and probably give the badge back. And I would
be in deep trouble.

My clothes were wet. I pulled off my hoodie
and jeans and took my little Swiss Army knife
out of my pocket.

I felt a bit down. Just a little sad.

I couldn't tell anyone that I could fly.
And I couldn't tell anyone how clever I'd been
to be able to get that fire started.

But then I cheered up.

I had done something kind.

And Samantha was happy. That was the
main thing.

I looked at myself in the mirror.

Okay, I was just about bald. It was a big loss.

But my hair had got the fire going. It was worth it.

I hoped that one day my good deed would pay off.

And it did. But that's another story.

STORY TWO

JUST A NIBBLE

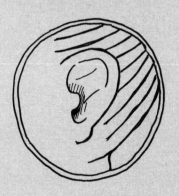

1

THE GOOD
THE BAD AND
THE DORK

There are people in your life who you like.

LIKE

MRS SNIPSTITCH
THE TUCKSHOP
LADY

MY COUSIN
BRETT

OUR TEACHER
JENNY

PUGWASH
- BRETT'S STINKY
DOG

And there are people in your life who you don't like.

DON'T LIKE

CRANKY
MRS BRIGGS
NEXT DOOR

MR LINDQUIST,
OUR DENTIST

MR WETHERS,
HEADMASTER

MR SPRANGLE,
MILK BAR OWNER
(MEAN)

My dad fits one of these.

I like him.

Even though he is a bit daggy. Even though he can be embarrassing.

Dad is the only other person in the world who can fly. So that makes him special.

No one knows Dad can fly. No one knows I can fly.

Because if anyone sees us, if *anything* sees us when we are flying, we will drop to our death.

So flying is a problem. And dying is a problem.

And when you share a problem with someone in matters of life and death, you understand each other.

Big time.

That's why me and Dad are close.

He is the best.

I love him.

SOME THINGS YOU SHOULD KNOW ABOUT **DAD**.

- Early signs of baldness. In denial. ⎯

- Mouth full of Dad jokes. ⎯⎯

- Good for talking to. Actually quite wise under all the Dad stuff. ⎯

- Overalls from job as a handyman. His business name is 'Mr Fix-ation'. Mum says it makes him sound ⎯ like a stalker.

- Little belly. ⎯⎯⎯

- Excellent at fixing things. ⎯

I love Dad. Dad loves me back.

But there are people you love who don't love you back.

Like a certain person called Samantha.

Who doesn't even know that I exist.

There are also people you can't stand. Like Jack.
Who I haven't even met.

I don't like him because I overheard Samantha
telling her girlfriend on the phone how he
nibbled her ear.

He nibbled her ear. Can you believe that?
I couldn't stop thinking about it. I was jealous.

In my mind I knew what Jack looked like.

The opposite to me in every way.

As you travel on life's journey you have to find

a way to handle all the people you meet.

I have developed some people-handling

strategies – skills that are useful.

STRATEGIES

MUM : BE SUPER NICE, PICK FLOWERS, ETC.

NEVER FAILS. SHE'S A PUSHOVER.

DAD : DO CHORES — CLEAN SHED, VAN, ETC.

WORTH IT ? NOT SURE.

MANDY CHOW: IGNORE MEANNESS

 JACK:

CHALLENGE TO A DUEL

DOESN'T WORK 🙁. SHE IGNORES <u>MY</u> IGNORING.

HAVEN'T ACTUALLY MET, BUT WHEN I DO...

 **SAMANTHA**: NIBBLE EAR. (APPARENTLY A GOOD STRATEGY.)

MAYBE I'D START BY INTRODUCING MYSELF...

In my life at the moment there are the good,

the bad and the beautiful.

Dad and Mum are good.

Jack and Mandy Chow are bad.

Samantha is beautiful.

And then there is me.

Ricky, the flying dork.

If only people could see me fly. Then everything would change.

I would be...

But I wasn't famous. Until I could fly and be seen flying, I would have to find another way to impress Samantha.

I couldn't just walk up to her at the car wash and say, 'Would you like your ear nibbled?'

I had to approach it another way.

Everything I had tried so far had failed to impress her.

I had tried to grow long hair so that I could look like Jack. But it didn't work because I had to cut it all off and use it to start a fire in the rain. But I couldn't tell her that I'd helped her.

So that failed.

And when I'd showed off at the car wash I'd just about killed myself.

So that failed.

Maybe I needed to try something really different. My mind started to wander.

And wonder.

2

NICE AND PRIVATE

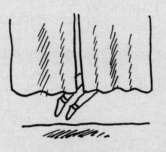

The answer to my problem happened out of the blue. Unexpectedly.

Dad and I were walking along a leafy track in the forest. I was thinking about Samantha. And her boyfriend, Jack.

It was a quiet, peaceful spot. I decided to ask Dad about girls.

We walked through the forest until we reached a creek.

I took a deep breath.

It was time to ask Dad for advice.

We put our backpacks down on the grassy bank.

'What have you got in there?' said Dad.

'Valuable supplies,' I said.

'What sort of valuable supplies?'

I stared at my backpack. I didn't want him to know what was inside it.

CONTENTS OF MY

 WATER BOTTLE

 MUM'S MEGA MARSHMALLOW MAPLE MUFFINS

 SANDWICHES

 SWISS ARMY KNIFE

HOPELESSLY BRUISED BANANA (WHOLE BAG A BIT BANANA-Y)

  SCRUNCHED-UP HOMEWORK AT BOTTOM OF BAG

PTERODACTYL FIGURINE (MISSING LEG)

 PTERODACTYL LEG

BACKPACK

COMIC

I needed to stop further questions about the backpack. Otherwise I would get a lecture about the absence of a compass, snakebite kit, bandages and dried fruit.

I used my foolproof method of distracting Dad.

Always answer a question with a question.

It gets you out of telling lies.

'What do you think about ear nibbling?' I said.

'Depends whose ear it is,' said Dad.

'Do you do it?' I asked.

'That's private information,' he said.

He had a sheepish look on his face. I could tell that he was a secret ear-nibbler.

The thought of Dad nibbling Mum's ear was disgusting.

Or maybe she nibbled his ear.

Even worse.

Life was full of disgusting things.

DISGUSTING THINGS

PARSNIP

BUCKET OF VOMIT

DEAD RAT I FOUND AT THE BOTTOM OF OUR GARDEN

MUM AND DAD EAR NIBBLING

Dad and I trudged on. We were heading uphill and I started to get tired.

'Just remember,' said Dad, 'flying is hard work. In order to keep yourself off the ground you have to be fit. Never fly when you are feeling weak. Never fly when your energy levels are low.'

I grinned. I didn't want him to think I was weak.

We were heading for a private spot I had chosen.

A place where no one would see us – White's Fall.

Dad was going to give me a flying lesson.

He wanted me to learn how to be sensible.

He didn't want me to kill myself by doing
something silly.

Suddenly I stopped.

'This is it,' I said. 'This is the place.'

I stared over the edge of White's Fall. It made me feel giddy.

'You are not ready for that yet,' said Dad. 'No way, not for years. Maybe never.'

I shivered. It was a long way down. I could see a mob of kangaroos far below. They looked like hopping fleas. I took a few steps back from the cliff. My knees were knocking.

Dad was right. I was definitely not ready to go flying at that height. It would be crazy to fly that high in broad daylight.

If just one person or creature saw me I would fall.

3
PRACTISING

NGGG

'It's a good place to practise,' said Dad.

'As long as we stay away from the cliff.'

'What will I do first?' I said.

'Hover,' he said.

Dad closed his eyes. If he saw me in the air

I would fall to the ground. We both knew that.

'Now go up higher,' said Dad.

It was hard work, but finally I reached a branch on a tree. I sat on it and looked down at Dad.

'Are you up?' said Dad.

'Yes.'

'Okay, now come down again.'

I plopped down at his feet and he opened his eyes.

Dad took a breath. I knew he was going to give me more advice.

'How do you become a good runner?' he said.

'Tell me,' I said.

'By running,' he said. 'You learn to run by running. You learn to play golf by playing golf. You learn to read by—'

I cut him off. 'Reading,' I said. 'I get it. You want me to practise, practise, practise.'

He nodded. 'It's more than that. You have to exercise. You have to exercise your brain as well as your muscles if you want to fly. Now let's see what you can do.'

I nodded and went back to work.

ASCENDING AND DESCENDING

CARRYING WEIGHTS

SOMERSAULTS

FOCUSING

MEDITATION

After hours of easy stuff, Dad put my backpack
into my hands.

'Fly up to the first branch on that tree again,'
he said. 'Then rest there for a bit and fly back
down with it.'

The tree had a towering, smooth trunk. The first
branch was way above my head.

Dad had more advice.

'You could never climb down from a tree with
a smooth trunk like that,' he said. 'I want you
to think about that. If busybodies came by,
you would be stuck up there.'

I weighed the backpack in my hands.

'Easy,' I said. 'Don't worry.'

'Don't get cocky,' said Dad. 'Heavy weights use up brain power. It's just like weight-lifting. You learn to lift weights by...'

'Lifting weights,' I said quickly.

He laughed and closed his eyes.

'Ricky going up,' I yelled.

'Ricky going up,' he replied.

Dad was right. I could feel my brain going into overload. It did need exercise. I had to really concentrate to get up there. I settled on the first branch of the gum tree and cradled the backpack on my knees.

'Safe,' I yelled down to Dad.

Dad opened his eyes and looked up.

'How was it?' he said.

'Heavy. I feel tired.'

'That's right,' said Dad. 'So just imagine how hard it would be to lift a person. You could both crash to the ground if you weren't fit enough. Or if someone saw you.'

'Okay,' I said. 'I get it.'

He was right. I was not up to lifting a person yet.

Suddenly I sensed another pair of eyes.

Hungry eyes.

It was a possum.

There was no way I could fly down from the tree while it was watching me.

'Shoo,' I said.

The possum stayed put. It could smell the food in my backpack. It wasn't going anywhere.

'Hello,' said a girl's voice.

I froze.

Someone had spoken. I was still sitting on the high branch up in the tree with my backpack in my lap. It was heavy and it hurt my hands and knees. I couldn't fly down because they would see me. And I couldn't drop the backpack because they would hear it.

'Hello,' said Dad.

I was stuck.

4

A DEAD DUCK

looked down from my high perch.

I couldn't take it in. My mind started to swirl.

The ground seemed to swim beneath my feet.

Was it really her?

I could hardly breathe. I felt faint, but I hung onto my perch desperately. Yes, it was her.

It was…

Samantha and her father were right underneath me.

I couldn't stop my hands trembling. I was stuck up the tree. They hadn't seen me yet.

I felt giddy.

I couldn't fly down because Samantha and her father might see me and I would fall like a dead duck at their feet.

I was still clutching the heavy backpack and it was digging into my lap.

Then an alarming sound sent shivers down my spine.

I heard Samantha's father speak.

'Hi,' he said to Dad. 'I didn't expect to see anyone here.'

'Neither did I,' said Dad.

'We have a problem,' said Samantha's father. 'We're looking for—'

'Jack,' said Samantha. 'He's lost in the forest somewhere. We have to find him before night comes. I love him so much.'

Dark, jealous thoughts seeped into my mind. She was looking for her boyfriend.

Samantha's father held her hand tightly and they walked carefully to the top of the cliff face and peered down.

'Jack isn't down there,' he said.

'Thank goodness,' said Samantha.

An eagle floated on the breeze, held in place by a current of air that bounced from the cliff face.

But I had no time to enjoy the view. My backpack was heavy. The branch was bending.

And the possum was making it hard for me to hang on.

Something had to give.

Dad heard the creaking branch. He realised what was happening, but he was helpless. He couldn't fly up to save me. He couldn't even get off the ground while Samantha and her father were watching.

'Drop it,' yelled Dad. 'Drop the backpack.'

Samantha and her father jumped in fright.

'How did you get up there?' Samantha's father yelled.

I had to think quickly. What could I say?

What explanation could I give? Crazy thoughts flitted through my head.

'I climbed up here,' I said.

It was a lie, but I couldn't tell him that I flew up there.

'Move in towards the trunk,' yelled Dad.

'The branch is going to break.'

'I can't. I'm scared,' I yelled.

'Don't move,' ordered Samantha's father.
He dropped his daughter's hand and ran over
to the tree.

'I'll get you down,' he yelled.

Dad put a hand on his shoulder and spoke to
Samantha and her father.

'Wait,' he said.

Then he said something I never thought he would
say to anyone. Not even Mum.

'Close your eyes, and Ricky will fly down,' said Dad.

5
BLOOD AND BONE

I couldn't believe my ears. Dad had sworn never to tell anyone that we could fly. He had made me promise. He was breaking his own vow. Telling our secret. That's how much he loved me, I guessed.

'Don't be stupid,' yelled Samantha's father.

He put his arms around the tree trunk and began to shin up. He was a good climber.

I was in deadly danger. I was shaking so much that I could hardly keep my balance. The branch gave a small squeak as the crack ran further along its length.

Dad knew that I could fly down. He didn't want Samantha's father to put himself in danger. He tried to stop him.

'Shut your eyes,' Dad shouted at Samantha and her father. 'He can fly if you don't look.'

'You fool,' yelled Samantha's father. 'The branch is going to break.'

'Please, just stop climbing and close your eyes,' said Dad.

'You're crazy,' he yelled, climbing higher.

Dad tried a different approach. 'Yes, I'm crazy,'

he yelled back. 'Woo-eee. Totally crazy.'

He was jumping around, trying to distract

Samantha's dad.

Samantha's dad stopped climbing and stared.
Dad had his attention, but he still had to stop
Samantha's dad getting any higher.

All of a sudden he had an idea. He dropped
to his knees and reached for my backpack,
which had fallen near his feet.

That's when I noticed Samantha wasn't near
the tree anymore.

She was backing away from the arguing men.

She was in deadly danger, but no one except me knew. Her father was trying to climb up the tree to save me.

And Dad was fishing around in my backpack. Then he started to throw things.

Precious things.

All the special bits and pieces from my backpack
flew through the air.

Sandwiches, homework, my Pterodactyl figurine.
He was trying to knock Samantha's father down.

Dad aimed carefully with the last item in the bag.

Mum's Mega Marshmallow Maple Muffin.

The deadly missile found its target.

Smash. Crash. Crack. Samantha's father screamed, and fell, right on top of Dad.

Samantha's father lay on the ground without moving. His eyes were closed.

He was out to it.

Then I heard Samantha's voice.

Dad was groaning. 'My leg,' he shouted. 'It's broken.' He shook Samantha's father, but there was no movement.

I looked around. Samantha was gone. There was no sign of her.

The branch creaked beneath me.

'Quick,' yelled Dad. 'The coast is clear. Get down from there.' He shut his eyes.

'Ricky coming down,' I screamed.

'Ricky coming down,' groaned Dad.

I flew to the ground as quickly as I could and landed with a thud right next to Dad.

'Are you okay?' I said.

Dad's leg looked terrible. It was bent the wrong way. And bleeding.

He could hardly move.

He pointed to his pack, which lay nearby. 'Get the bandage,' he groaned.

I quickly took the bandage out of his pack and wrapped it around his leg.

He winced.

I pointed to Samantha's father. 'What about him?' I said.

'Unconscious,' said Dad.

'Help.'

A frightened voice was calling.

'Help.' There it was again.

I ran over to the cliff.

I peered over the edge.

There was no way I could climb down.

'Don't move,' I screamed to Samantha.
'I'll get you.'

'No,' shouted Dad. 'I'll do it.' He winced again
with pain.

'You can't,' I said.

'Don't fly down to her,' said Dad. 'If she looks
at you it will be death for you both.'

No one could survive a fall like that.

If Samantha stumbled off the ledge she would die for sure. For a second I even wished that Jack would show up. I didn't want her to die.

'Shut your eyes,' I shouted down to Samantha.

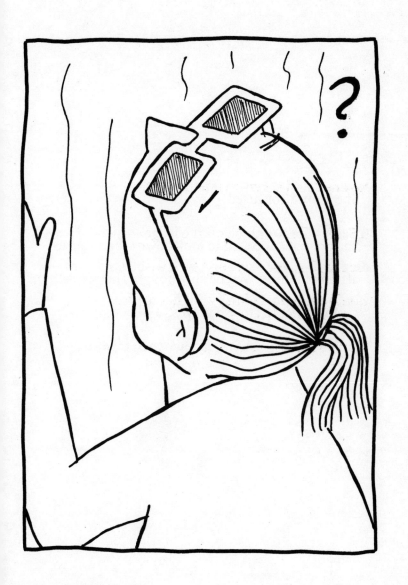

She looked confused.

You are not supposed to look down when you are afraid of falling. Maybe she thought that was why I wanted her to close her eyes.

The cliff went straight down. A stone broke away from the small ledge and spun into the air. It took ages to disappear into the trees in the valley below.

I had to do something.

'Close your eyes, Samantha,' I yelled again. 'Please close your eyes.'

'Ricky going down,' I yelled.

'No,' shrieked Dad. He instinctively closed his eyes. Then he groaned, 'Don't do it. Don't do it.'

6

SUNGLASSES

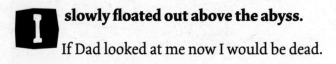 **I** slowly floated out above the abyss.

If Dad looked at me now I would be dead.

I lowered myself towards Samantha. 'Close your eyes,' I yelled at her. 'Don't look.'

I knew I was doomed. She would watch me plunge the whole way, until I splattered onto the ground. Headfirst.

But there was no time for scary thoughts. I was descending rapidly. Quicker and quicker. Faster and faster. I landed hard, falling in a crumpled heap next to Samantha on the narrow ledge.

'Close your eyes,' I said. 'Please close your eyes.'

I couldn't see whether she had or not. The ledge we were on was starting to crumble.

I grabbed her and lifted her like a fireman carrying a child out of a burning house.

I rose off the ledge. I was holding her in midair. She was so heavy. I thought I was going to drop her. I couldn't seem to rise further. I was just hovering, not going up, not going down.

Then her sunglasses dislodged.

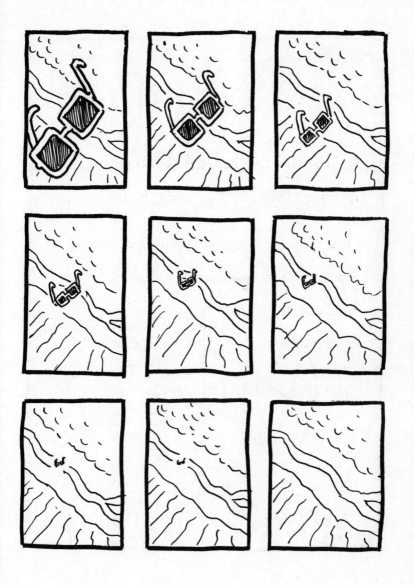

Then, just as I thought that all was lost, I lifted
a few centimetres. And then a few more. We were
going up.

I rose into the air, holding her tightly in my arms.
Up, up, up. Now there was nothing below us but
empty air. Only certain death was beneath our
feet. But slowly, slowly, slowly, we ascended.

The edge of the cliff was just above my head.
But I was tired – so tired. I had no strength left.

'Ricky,' said a voice. 'Are you there? Are you still
alive?'

It was Dad. He had dragged himself over to the edge. His eyes were closed. He couldn't see me carrying Samantha in midair. But he knew how steep the cliff was.

One look, one glance from Dad, and I would plunge to my death, taking Samantha with me.

Dad called out. His voice echoed in the valley below.

'If you have that girl, you will have to concentrate. Give it all you have got.'

All I could do was gasp.

I made one last desperate effort.

'Up,' I said to myself. 'Up, up, up.'

My head was aching. The pain was terrible. I felt as if my skull had been whacked with a hammer. I was pouring with sweat.

Up, up, just a few centimetres more. That was all I needed. My feet were level with the edge of the cliff, but I was still hanging in midair. I floated in, above solid earth. The soles of my shoes were just above the grass. Samantha was still in my arms.

I had made it.

Samantha's father stirred. He moaned and lifted his head and stared straight at me. I plopped to the ground in front of him.

He stumbled over to his daughter and hugged her.

'The boy saved me,' said Samantha. 'He carried me up the cliff. It felt so gentle. Like floating in a hot-air balloon. He saved my life.'

Samantha's father took a step towards me and held out his hand. 'I will be forever grateful, son,' he said. He stared down into the abyss and added, 'But I don't know how you did it. There is no track.'

I turned away and rushed over to Dad, who had crawled into the shade of the tree. 'Are you okay, Dad?' I said.

He was holding his injured leg and I could see it was painful. But he managed a grin.

'You were lucky,' he whispered. 'They didn't see you.'

'She opened her eyes,' I said to Dad. 'She saw me fly. And I didn't fall. I'll bet her stupid boyfriend, Jack, can't match that.'

Just then there was a noise in the nearby bushes.

We all turned our heads to see who it was.

'Jack,' yelled Samantha's father.

'Darling,' yelled Samantha. 'It's you.'

Dad smiled at me. 'Well, I'll be darned,' he said.

I didn't know whether to be happy or sad.
I guess I was both. Samantha's dog scampered
over to her, trailing his lead behind him. It was
attached to a shoulder harness. A seeing-eye-dog
harness.

So that's why I didn't fall to my death even
though her eyes were open. She couldn't see.
She was blind.

Samantha hugged Jack and then turned back
to me.

I could feel her ear pressing against my skin.

It was a lovely soft ear.

'Thank you so much for saving my life,' she said.

'You are amazing.'

Samantha liked me.

We were going to be friends. I just knew it.

And I didn't even have to nibble her ear.

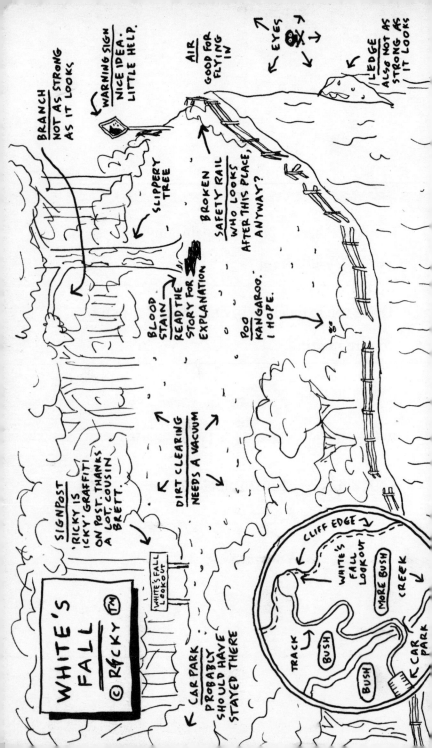